Treasury of
Bedtime Stories

pi kids® publications international, ltd.

Cover illustrated by Renee Graef
Title page illustrated by Veronica Vasylenko

Stories adapted by Jennifer Boudart, Caleb Burroughs,
Brian Conway, Jamie Elder, and Lisa Harkrader

Louis Weber, C.E.O.
Publications International, Ltd.
7373 North Cicero Avenue, Lincolnwood, Illinois 60712

Ground Floor, 59 Gloucester Place
London W1U 8JJ

Customer Service: 1-800-595-8484 or customer_service@pilbooks.com

www.pilbooks.com

8 7 6 5 4 3 2 1

ISBN-13: 978-1-4127-5925-0
ISBN-10: 1-4127-5925-0

CONTENTS

Puss in Boots

Adapted from the English fairy tale
Illustrated by Jacqueline East

Once upon a time, there lived a clever cat named Puss. One day, Puss lost his owner, a poor farmer. Puss was alone, with nobody to take care of or to take care of him.

Puss decided to find a new owner, and chose the farmer's son. Puss approached the young man and politely said, "Please take me home with you."

"I can't help you," said the young man.

"I am no trouble," said Puss. "I'll even help you. Just give me boots and an old sack."

"All right," laughed the young man.

Puss followed the young man home,
where they found a pair of boots and a sack.

"I don't understand what you want with
boots and an old sack," the young man said.

Puss smiled, put the boots on, picked up
the sack, and headed into the forest.

As he walked, Puss gathered grass. He
filled the sack with the green grass he picked.
Finding a tree, Puss dropped the sack, closed
his eyes, and pretended to be asleep.

Soon, a rabbit hopped by, smelling the
fresh grass. The rabbit crawled inside the sack
and—*THWAP!*—Puss snatched it right up!

With the rabbit in the sack and the sack
on his back, Puss headed to the king's castle.

Arriving at the castle, Puss was ushered into the great throne room.

"Your Highness," the cat said. "I have brought you a gift from my master, the Duke of Cataclaws."

"What is it?" the king asked, and Puss presented him with the splendid rabbit.

The king was glad that the Duke of Cataclaws would send such a fine gift. Little did the king know that there was no Duke of Cataclaws, or that he'd been tricked by a cat.

The rest of the week, Puss gave the king gifts. He brought tasty trout, fat pheasants, and plump partridges. As Puss gave each gift, he said it was from the Duke of Cataclaws.

One day the king decided to take a ride through his kingdom. He took with him his beautiful daughter, the princess.

Puss hurried back home to his master. He told the young man, "You must take off your clothes and jump into the pond by the road."

As the young man hopped in the pond, the royal carriage came down the road. Puss ran to meet it, crying, "Help! The Duke of Cataclaws has been tossed into the water!"

"The Duke of Cataclaws?" asked the king. "Guards, help this man, lest he drown!"

As the king's guards rushed to the young man's aid, Puss sneaked up to the king's carriage and poked his head inside.

"Hello," Puss greeted the princess.

"I am worried about the Duke of Cataclaws," she said. "What happened?"

"He was robbed by hoodlums," Puss said. "The robbers took all of his money. But the king's guards have saved him."

The guards brought the wet young man to the carriage. "Find the duke a dry set of clothes," the king ordered.

"Father, can the duke ride in the carriage with us?" the princess asked the king.

Before the young man knew what was going on, Puss answered, "The duke accepts."

With that, the cat ran ahead of the king's carriage, for he had more work to do.

After running and running, Puss came to some farmers.

"Hello, my fine fellows," said the cat. "You look like you are working hard."

"We work these fields for the giant who lives in yonder castle," said a farmer.

"If we don't work hard, he'll gobble us up," said another farmer.

"About that giant," said Puss, "the king has just named him the Duke of Cataclaws. Now, the king's carriage will come by soon. Make sure you tell the king that the castle belongs to the Duke of Cataclaws."

Next, Puss ran to the castle. For his plan to work, he still had to deal with the giant.

At the castle, Puss found a terrible giant.

"I have heard many great things about you," Puss said. "I have heard that you can turn yourself into any animal that you wish."

"It's true," said the giant. "I can turn into a lion, a bear, or even a great whale."

"But I doubt you could turn into a tiny animal, like a mouse," Puss said.

To prove Puss wrong, the giant turned himself into a mouse — which the cat gobbled right up.

Soon the carriage arrived. Puss said, "Welcome to the castle of the Duke of Cataclaws!" The young man smiled at his cat and his new home.

Rocking-Horse Land

Adapted from the fairy tale by Laurence Housman
Illustrated by Bandelin-Dacey Studios

There once lived a prince named Little Prince Freedling. One morning, Little Prince Freedling rose out of bed like a rocket, as it was a special day.

It was his fifth birthday, and all of the church bells and grandfather clocks in the kingdom announced it at this early hour.

But the prince did not make it past the foot of his bed, for there he found piles of beautifully wrapped birthday gifts.

The first gift that Freedling unwrapped was from his fairy godmother. The note attached to the gift read: "Break me and I shall turn into something else." And the toy did just that. What started out as a top changed once Freedling broke it. In just one hour, the toy became a jump rope, a ship, building blocks, a jigsaw puzzle, a drum, a kaleidoscope, a whistle, and a thousand other things. It became a kite, and its string broke. Off it flew, never to be seen again.

Little Prince Freedling looked for another gift. He found one by his window: a great, golden rocking horse.

Freedling ran to the window and threw his arms around the horse's neck. The horse's big eyes shone so bright, they almost seemed alive. The prince climbed on the horse's back and spent the day there, chasing dragons and villains in his bedroom.

That night, Freedling woke up longing to see his rocking horse once more. The prince was shocked to find that the horse was not where he had left it. Instead, it had crossed his bedroom and stood staring out the window into the dark, dark night.

Freedling saw that its eyes were full of tears that shone in the starlight.

"Why are you crying?" Freedling asked.

To Freedling's surprise, the rocking horse answered, "Because I am not free. Won't you let me go?" it asked.

"Will you come back?" asked Freedling.

The horse said, "My name is Rollonde. My brothers call me to Rocking-Horse Land. Look in my mane and find the one black hair. Pluck it and wrap it around your finger. As long as you have that hair, you are my master, and I shall return to you each morning."

The prince threw open the window and called, "Rollonde, go to Rocking-Horse Land, but please return to me come morning!"

Rollonde spent the night in the sky. In the morning, he returned to the prince.

A year passed, with Freedling riding Rollonde each day and setting him free each night. Soon the prince awoke to his sixth birthday. The bells and clocks called to him. The gifts sat wrapped at the foot of his bed. The first that Freedling opened was from his fairy godmother. This gift turned out to be a parrot. When the prince pulled the bird's tail, it became a striped lizard. When the prince pulled the lizard's tail, it became a border collie. But when he pulled the pup's tail, it became a Manx cat, which has no tail. Seeing this, the prince looked for his next gift.

The king presented the prince with the finest young stallion in the kingdom.

Prince Freedling spent that day riding his new horse. In fact, he completely forgot about his rocking horse, Rollonde.

That night, as Freedling fell alseep, he heard a crying from beside his bed. The prince looked up to find Rollonde standing there, tears streaming down his face.

"You have a real horse of your own. May I go to Rocking-Horse Land for good?" wept Rollonde.

Freedling threw open the shutters and let Rollonde gallop off into the night sky.

The prince watched the horse go to Rocking-Horse Land. Then he took the black hair from his finger and let it float away, too.

When Little Prince Freedling had grown up to become King Freedling, it was the fifth birthday of his own son, the new prince. Beautifully wrapped gifts covered the prince's bedroom, including a beautiful, golden rocking-horse colt.

The king knelt down and saw that the colt looked so much like his own beloved rocking horse.

He searched its mane until he found a black hair. Plucking the hair, the king gently wrapped it around the prince's finger, sure that the prince would take good care of the son of his old friend, Rollonde.

The Nightingale

Adapted from the fairy tale by Hans Christian Andersen
Illustrated by Robin Moro

The Emperor of China lived in a vast and magnificent palace. Its rooms were vast. Its windows were draped in silk. Its floors displayed the finest Persian rugs. Its furniture was made from the rarest woods by the best craftsmen. And its gardens were tended by one hundred skilled gardeners.

One gardener told visitors, "I will show you the most beautiful thing in China." In a stand of trees was a plain, gray bird. Visitors wondered what was so beautiful until the nightingale sang its glorious music.

Because of the nightingale's singing, visitors would leave thinking only of the bird. They would return home and tell their friends and families about the nightingale.

This meant that more people flocked to the palace, all to see the nightingale. Every single visitor loved to hear the bird's song.

Yet the palace where the nightingale lived belonged to a person who had not heard the nightingale. You see, the Emperor was old, and hardly ever ventured outside.

One day, a letter came from the Emperor of Japan. "I have heard of this nightingale," the letter said. "I would very much like to visit and hear its song with my own ears."

But the Emperor of China had not heard the nightingale. He asked his men, "Where is the nightingale? Find it and bring it to me!"

The Emperor's men searched the palace, behind drapes and under rugs and on top of furniture, but could not find the nightingale.

The Emperor's men searched the palace gardens, looking among the plants and fruit trees, but could not find the nightingale.

Then, one of the gardeners said, "I know where the nightingale lives."

The gardener led the Emperor's men to the stand of trees where they found the plain, gray bird. The nightingale sang and the men knew they had found what they were seeking.

The men returned to the palace. Seeing the plain, gray bird, the Emperor asked, "What is so special about this nightingale?"

Before anyone could answer, a trumpet sounded. The Emperor of Japan had arrived! The guards rushed out to meet the visitor. The Chinese Emperor quickly prepared to present the famed bird to his fellow ruler.

The Emperor of Japan was led in. Seeing the plain, gray bird, he asked, "Is this the nightingale of which I have heard?"

The Emperor of China, not having heard the bird either, was equally confused.

Yet as the two men listened, the plain, gray nightingale broke into beautiful song.

The Japanese Emperor stayed in China for some time to hear the nightingale sing. The two rulers sat and listened to the bird's glorious melody all day and all night.

One day, the Emperor of Japan said, "Its song is so lovely, but it is a pity that the nightingale must look so very plain."

This made the Emperor of China sad. This creature deserved to look as beautiful as it sounded. He ordered that a gold cage be made for the nightingale. From the cage hung bells of silver and ribbons of silk.

When the Japanese Emperor was to leave, he said, "I will find a way to thank you for sharing the nightingale with me."

Soon the Emperor of Japan sent his gift. The Emperor of China opened it to find an artificial nightingale that was more beautiful than the real nightingale. It was covered in diamonds and sapphires and rubies.

The real beauty came when the bird was wound up. The Emperor turned the crank on the side of the artificial nightingale and was treated to the song that came from inside the bird. This bird sounded as good as the real nightingale!

But the real nightingale did not like the new bird. This bird only sang waltzes, and not nightingale songs. The real nightingale left its cage and flew back to the garden.

"I wonder where the nightingale went," said the Emperor of China.

"This new bird sings just as sweetly, and it looks more beautiful than the plain, gray nightingale," said one of his men.

"With this bird, we always know that waltzes will be sung. We never knew what the nightingale might sing," said another.

But one night, as the new nightingale sang one of its waltzes, the Emperor heard peculiar sounds come from the bird. There was a whizz, and a crack, and a whirr. With that, the artificial nightingale stopped singing.

The Emperor's best craftsmen could do nothing. The new nightingale was broken.

Time passed, with no nightingale music to fill the air. The people of China were full of sorrow. The Emperor would not leave his bed. He became ill, missing the song of his beloved bird.

Then one morning from outside the Emperor's window came the sweetest song. On a branch sat the real nightingale. The bird had heard of the Emperor's illness and had come to sing to him out of love, for the Emperor had once loved the nightingale.

As the nightingale sang, the Emperor began to feel better. The Emperor thanked the bird who now sat by his bed. That is where the nightingale stayed for the rest of its days.

Baba Yaga

Adapted from the traditional Russian folktale
Illustrated by Nan Brooks

In the land of Russia, there once lived a beautiful girl named Vasilissa. Surrounded by her mother and father, who was a wealthy merchant, Vasilissa lived a very happy life—until her mother fell ill.

One night Vasilissa's mother called her daughter to her bedside. Vasilissa ran to her mother and asked how she might help.

Vasilissa's mother said, "I will not be with you much longer. Take this doll. It will protect you from danger." Vasilissa kissed her mother one last time and took the doll.

With Vasilissa's mother now gone, her father found a new wife. Because he was wealthy, many women tried to win his love. One woman, who had a daughter of her own, was especially mean. Sadly, this was the woman Vasilissa's father married.

The woman and her daughter were envious of Vasilissa's beauty. They also hated the fact that Vasilissa's father loved her so. Because of their jealousy, the two made Vasilissa do the dirtiest household chores.

"You aren't so pretty scrubbing the floor, are you?" said her wicked stepmother.

"Your clothes aren't so fine covered in mop water, are they?" said her stepsister.

"I have a plan to rid us of Vasilissa once and for all!" the jealous stepmother said to her daughter one day.

"Our fire is out," the stepmother said to Vasilissa. "Go to Baba Yaga's for more fire."

Vasilissa shivered with fear. She had heard about Baba Yaga, a witch who lived in the forest. Baba Yaga's house stood on giant chicken legs. Baba Yaga ate people! Yet Vasilissa did as she was told and headed into the forest, carrying her doll. Soon Vasilissa arrived at Baba Yaga's house, where the old witch asked her what she wanted.

"I just need to borrow a bit of fire," Vasilissa replied.

"Well, come inside," cackled Baba Yaga.

Vasilissa climbed into Baba Yaga's house and became scared by what she saw. There were cawing ravens and hissing snakes. There were bones and creatures in jars.

"If you want to take a bit of fire, you'll have to do these things," said Baba Yaga, handing Vasilissa a list of chores.

With that, Baba Yaga left. Vasilissa knew she would never finish the chores. But when she turned around, she saw that her doll had come to life! Not only was the doll alive, it had already cleaned Baba Yaga's entire house, and had done the rest of the chores, too.

"Thank you, little doll," Vasilissa said.

The chores done, Vasilissa set the table and made supper before Baba Yaga returned. The witch had hoped the chores wouldn't be done, for then she would have eaten the girl.

"Very well," said Baba Yaga. "You may take a bit of fire home. Now get going!"

Vasilissa hurried home. When she arrived with the fire, Vasilissa found that her stepmother and stepsister were gone!

"You are home!" said her father. "I was so angry when I learned that you had been sent to Baba Yaga's. I made that woman and her daughter leave."

From then on, father and daughter and doll lived happily ever after.

The Boy Who Cried Wolf

Adapted from the fable by Aesop
Illustrated by Jon Goodell

Once there was a little village called Schaffenburg. Schaffenburg was much like any other little village, except for one thing—its many sheep. The village had so many sheep that the woolly creatures outnumbered the people!

These sheep were famous for what they provided—wool. They had the finest wool in the land. People came from far and wide to get things made from Schaffenburg wool.

Because they depended on the sheep's wool, the villagers took extra care to protect the sheep from harm. There were many wild beasts that would like nothing more than a sheep to eat—bears and lions and wolves.

To keep these animals from eating their precious sheep, the villagers trusted a boy to take good care of the flocks. This boy was named Wolfgang.

Each morning the boy gathered the sheep into one flock. Then he would lead them through the fields and pastures until he found the greenest grass. When the sheep were thirsty, Wolfgang led them to babbling brooks of water.

One day, Wolfgang began to daydream. He imagined that a wolf was after his flock, and that he bravely fought it off.

This daydream got him thinking: What would happen if a wolf really *did* come after his sheep? In all his days as the shepherd boy, Wolfgang had never had to deal with a wild animal. He was just a boy, and no match for a hungry, growling, prowling wolf!

Worried about what might happen if a wolf *did* attack the flock, Wolfgang wanted to see if the villagers would come to his aid.

His hand up to his mouth, Wolfgang called out in his most frightened voice, "Help! A wolf! A wolf!"

As Wolfgang had hoped, the people of the village came running to help. The village band dropped its tubas and accordions. The tavern girls dropped their mugs and plates. The farmers dropped their plows and milk buckets. Soon the entire village was in the pasture, hoping to save poor Wolfgang and his sheep from a wolf that was not there.

"I heard Wolfgang cry 'Wolf!'" said the tuba player. "I cut short my polka."

"I heard Wolfgang call," said a tavern girl. "I left my customers to come help."

"I heard Wolfgang crying that there was a wolf," said a farmer. "Why, I knocked over a morning's worth of milk as I ran to help!"

As the people of the village came to his rescue, Wolfgang found it funny. He laughed as the tuba player waddled along. He giggled as the tavern girl tripped over her apron. He howled as the farmer's hat flew off his head.

Alas, the people of the village did not find the prank as funny as Wolfgang did.

"There's no wolf?" asked the tubist.

"Wolfgang lied!" said the tavern girl.

"He's in trouble!" said the schoolmarm.

The farmer scolded, "You have lied to us. If a wolf attacks your sheep, you shouldn't expect us to come to your rescue."

Wolfgang held his head in shame. He had done wrong. He would never lie again.

Once the people of the village had left, Wolfgang sat down upon the grassy hill. As Wolfgang was thinking about his lie and the trouble it had caused, you would never believe what crept up behind him….

That's right—a real-life WOLF!

The beast chased the lambs, hungrily licking its lips. The snarling animal scattered the ewes, snapping its jaws. The growling canine stormed up the hill, glaring at poor Wolfgang with its glowing, yellow eyes.

Wolfgang didn't know what to do. So he ran. And he screamed and yelled for help.

"Help! Help!" Wolfgang cried. "A wolf! A wolf! Please save me from this awful wolf!"

Wolfgang dashed into the village. He ran down the streets of Schaffenburg, crying out that a wolf was after his sheep. Just as the farmer had warned, nobody came to help.

"He is lying," said the schoolmarm.

"Fiddlesticks," said the tavern girl. "That Wolfgang is trying to trick us."

The tuba player kept playing his polka, sure that Wolfgang wasn't telling the truth.

As the people of Schaffenburg went about their daily business, that wolf chased off the entire flock of sheep!

That day, Wolfgang learned that nobody believes a liar, even when he tells the truth.

Tom Sawyer

Adapted from the novel by Mark Twain
Illustrated by David Austin Clar

It was a sunny, summer Saturday and all was right with the world. St. Petersburg basked in the warmth of the sun. Birds sang. The laughter of the town's children, playing games of tag and leapfrog, echoed among the trees and red-brick homes.

Yes, all was right with the world — for everyone but Tom Sawyer.

Poor Tom watched his friends frolic and run. He watched the mighty steamboats chug up and down the muddy river. But watch was all Tom could do, for he had a fence to paint.

"Buffalo girls, won't you come out tonight, come out tonight, come out tonight?"

As he stood painting the fence, Tom heard a voice singing a funny song. The voice was getting closer and closer when Tom recognized who it was. It was his friend Jim!

"Jim!" Tom said, an idea in his head. "I bet you'd like to paint this fence, huh?"

"Oh, Tom," said Jim, "I don't believe I can do that. Your Aunt Polly warned me you would try to get me to do your work."

"This is hardly work at all," said Tom. "It's fun! I'll sit and read that comic book of yours while you paint the fence. Why I'll even show you my sore toe."

A sore toe isn't something you see every day. Especially a sore toe that was wrapped in a bandage. Jim agreed to help paint the fence for a quick peek—just one, small peek—at Tom's sore toe.

"This sure is a funny comic book," Tom laughed. He watched Jim paint away.

Just then a voice called from the house. "Tom Sawyer," it said, "I told you to paint that fence by yourself!" It was Aunt Polly!

As Aunt Polly came roaring out the front door, Jim scooted down the street, his comic book in his hand. Not so quickly, Tom picked up his brush and paint bucket and got back to his work.

Tom began to think of the fun he would be having if it weren't for Aunt Polly and her fence. He could be on some wild adventure, or watching the steamboats chug past.

As Tom thought of the steamboats that cruised the mighty Mississippi, he *heard* a steamboat—and it sounded awfully close.

Ding-dong! Toot-toot!

Tom saw Ben Rogers pretending to be the grand steamboat, the *Big Missouri.*

"Starboard!" Ben yelled, turning his imaginary boat's wheel. "Men, we're taking on water! Stop her, sir! *Ting-a-ling! Toot-toot!*"

Tom tried to ignore all of the fun Ben was having. It was hard to do.

"*Toot-toot!* Hi there, Tom," Ben said.

Tom pretended his friend wasn't there.

"You have to work today, huh?" asked Ben, holding a crisp, red apple. "Too bad. I'm going swimming. I bet you'd rather work."

"Work?" Tom asked, a plan in his head. "This isn't work. Painting is loads of fun!"

"I'd like to try," said Ben. "It's not every day that you get to paint. Can I paint a bit?"

"I can't let you," Tom said. "You see, my Aunt Polly is awful set on how she wants her fence painted. You might mess it all up."

But by now, Ben Rogers wanted to paint that old fence more than anything in the whole world.

Ben handed his apple to Tom. And Tom pretended to be sad as he handed the brush to Ben. But deep inside, Tom was happy to get out of the work.

Soon, Tom was surrounded by all of the children of St. Petersburg. They saw how Ben wanted to paint. *They* wanted to paint, too!

Tom sat munching his apple, planning how he would trick the rest of the children.

Once Ben Rogers was done, Tom let Billy Fisher paint — after Billy handed over his new kite. Once Billy was tired, Tom gave Johnny Miller the chance to paint for a rat and a piece of string.

Soon the happiest boy in St. Petersburg was Tom Sawyer. He now had a jaw harp, a piece of blue glass, a toy cannon, a key, a piece of chalk, a bottle cap, a toy soldier, a tadpole, a kitten, a brilliant brass doorknob, a dog collar without a dog, and an orange peel.

Yes, Tom was the happiest boy in town, sitting in the shade while his friends painted.

The North Wind

Adapted from the Norse folktale
Illustrated by Beth Foster Wiggins

In the land of Norway, there once lived a poor widow who had a son named Ivar. Ivar's mother was often sick. One day she said, "I am not feeling well. Could you please get some grain so that we can eat?"

Ivar, a loving son, said that he would. He set off to get a basketful of grain.

As Ivar walked home, along came the North Wind. Blustering and blowing, the North Wind blew away all of Ivar's grain.

Ivar decided he would ask the North Wind to give the grain back.

The journey to the North Wind's house was long. Ivar finally arrived at the door of the North Wind and called out, "Hello!"

The North Wind answered back in his blustery voice, "Hello to you! Thank you for coming to visit me. How can I help you?"

"Will you give me back the grain that you blew out of my basket?" Ivar asked. "My mother and I are so poor and hungry."

"I do not have your grain," said the North Wind. "But I will give you a magic tablecloth. Say, 'Cloth, spread yourself,' and it will serve you all sorts of good food."

Ivar took the tablecloth and left. It was such a long trip that he stopped at an inn.

Inside the inn, Ivar placed the tablecloth on a table and said, "Cloth, spread yourself." The tablecloth did as the North Wind had promised. There on the table was an entire delicious meal laid out: juicy roast beef, ripe vegetables, a heaping cake, and hearty bread.

Ivar was amazed. He ate and ate.

Another person had seen the tablecloth do its magic and was just as amazed. The innkeeper, a bad man, had watched the trick.

Once Ivar was fast asleep the innkeeper took the magic tablecloth from the boy's sack. He put a regular tablecloth in its place.

The next day, Ivar awoke. Not knowing he'd been tricked, the boy headed home.

When Ivar arrived at home, he told his mother of the magic tablecloth. "We'll have plenty to eat!" he said.

But when the boy put the tablecloth on the table, nothing happened! Not one piece of food appeared. Ivar was disappointed. The tablecloth had worked its magic the day before. Why wasn't it working now?

"The only thing to do is for me to go back to the North Wind's house and tell him what is wrong," Ivar told his mother.

With that, Ivar walked and walked until he again arrived at the North Wind's house, and said, "You've given me this worthless tablecloth. It will not do what you said."

"Why don't you take this magic bank?" the North Wind offered. "If you tell the bank, 'Rain, bank! Make money!' it will make you gold coins."

So Ivar took the magic bank and headed home. Once again, he stopped at the inn for the night. Inside, Ivar took out the bank and said, "Rain, bank! Make money!" The bank began to spit out shiny coins of gold.

But once Ivar was asleep, the innkeeper sneaked into the boy's room and took the magic bank from his sack. The innkeeper replaced the magic bank with a regular one.

Not knowing he'd been tricked, Ivar took his sack and headed home the next day.

Once home, Ivar said, "Rain, bank! Make money!" but nothing happened!

This time, Ivar was very disappointed. The tablecloth hadn't worked, and now the bank didn't work. "The only thing to do is for me to go back to the North Wind's house and tell him what is wrong," Ivar said.

With that, the boy walked and walked, until he arrived at the door of the North Wind. He knocked on the door and said, "This bank will not do what you said."

"All I have left is this magic rope," said the North Wind. "Say, 'Rope, rope, tie on,' it will tie up whatever you like. And watch out for that sneaky innkeeper."

Ivar took the magic rope and stopped at the same inn as before. Suspicious, Ivar climbed into bed and pretended to sleep.

As soon as he heard Ivar's snoring, the innkeeper crept into the boy's room, intent on stealing whatever the boy had in his sack. Just as the innkeeper was about to pick up the rope, Ivar shouted, "Rope, rope, tie on!"

Like a snake, the rope wrapped itself around the innkeeper. It tied up his hands and feet. "Help!" the innkeeper cried. "Let me loose!" Ivar only let the innkeeper go once he had his magic tablecloth and bank back. Then Ivar headed home, where he and his mother were never poor or hungry again.

Clever Manka

Adapted from the Czech folktale
Illustrated by Pat Hoggan

Long ago in Ceskoslovensko, there lived a wealthy farmer who always got the best of his poor neighbors. One of these was a poor shepherd whose only delight was his clever and beautiful daughter, Manka.

The shepherd had done work for the farmer, who promised him a calf in return. But the farmer would not part with the calf.

So the shepherd went before the mayor. The mayor said to the shepherd, "I will ask both you and the farmer a riddle. Whoever answers correctly gets the calf."

100

The mayor turned to the farmer. "What is the fastest thing in the world? What is the sweetest? What is the richest?" he asked.

The farmer smiled, for he thought he knew the answers. "The fastest is my mare, for nothing can pass her. My honey is the sweetest thing I've ever tasted. And the chest of gold coins I've been saving is the richest."

Next, Manka told her father how to respond. He said, "The fastest is thought, for it can run any distance in no time at all. The sweetest is sleep, when one is sad and tired. The richest is the ground, for out of it come all the riches of the earth."

The shepherd had won the calf!

The shepherd confessed that it was his daughter who had known the answers.

The mayor turned to Manka and said, "I think I would like to marry you. Please come see me tomorrow. But come neither at day nor at night, neither riding nor walking, and neither clothed nor unclothed."

The next day Manka left at dawn, as the night was done and the day hadn't come. She wrapped herself in a fishnet and came with one leg on a goat's back and one leg on the road. The mayor smiled. It wasn't day or night, a fishnet is not clothing, and clever Manka neither rode nor walked. The mayor married Manka that very day.

The two had been married for a short while when the mayor said, "Manka, you cannot use your cleverness to meddle with any of the cases I judge. If you give advice to someone who comes to me, I'll put you out of my house and send you home to your father."

One day a man came out of the mayor's house looking sad. Manka, who had a kind heart, asked the man what was wrong.

"I told the mayor my problem," he said. "I owned a mare who had her foal at market. The foal ran under another farmer's wagon. That man claimed that it was *his* foal. I came to the mayor hoping to get my foal back."

"Did he give it to you?" Manka asked.

"No," the man said. "He was thinking of something else while I talked. He didn't listen, and gave the foal to the other man."

Manka was sad that this farmer had lost what was rightfully his. She was angry that her husband had not made a wise choice. She decided to use her cleverness to help, even though her husband had told her not to.

Manka told him, "Come back later with your fishing pole. Sit in front of our house, casting the line onto the dusty road. When the mayor asks how you catch fish on a dusty road, tell him that it's as easy to catch fish on a dusty road as it is for a wagon to have a foal. You must not say that I told you this."

Later, the farmer came to the mayor's house with his fishing pole. He cast the line onto the dusty road. The mayor asked, "Why are you fishing on the dusty road?"

The man said, "It is as easy to fish on a dusty road as it is for a wagon to have a foal."

The mayor realized that he had been wrong and said, "That foal belongs to you. Who was clever enough to tell you to this?"

The farmer forgot what Manka had asked and blurted out her name.

The mayor told Manka, "What I did I tell you about giving advice? You must go back to your father, but you may take one thing from my house." Then he went to bed.

The next morning, the mayor awoke somewhere other than his own bed. He was in the shepherd's small cottage!

Seeing Manka, the mayor asked, "Why have you taken me from my own house?"

Manka replied, "You told me that I could take one thing from your house. And because I love you, I took you. That is why you are here in my father's cottage."

The mayor thought about this and began to laugh. "Manka," he said, "you are far more clever than I am. Let's go home."

From that day forth, the mayor always accepted Manka's clever advice when he had a case that was especially puzzling.

The Bell of Justice

Adapted from the ballad by Henry Wadsworth Longfellow
Illustrated by Jon Goodell

here once was a small and humble town called Atri.

One day King John's procession came through Atri. When King John reached the town square, he said, "By royal order, a bell shall hang here. When anyone is wronged, ring the bell. When this Bell of Justice is rung, the town's judge shall correct whatever wrong has been done." And so a bell hung in the square and the king's orders were obeyed.

For many years, the Bell of Justice rang when wrongs were done. When livestock was stolen, the farmer rang the bell. When a grandmother's fruit pie was swiped, she rang the bell. When a child was bullied, he or she rang the bell. In every case, the judge would bring justice to those who had done wrong.

Yet Atri's love for the Bell of Justice ended. After many years of not being used, the bell rusted, and its rope fell off.

Although Atri had forgotten about the Bell of Justice, the town's judge had not. He called to one man and said, "Please go into the woods and get a vine. We will tie the vine to the bell so that it can be rung again."

Since the rule of King John, other things had changed besides the Bell of Justice. During King John's reign, there had been a gallant knight called the Knight of Atri. Tales of his adventures were still told. Yet knights, just like bells, grow rusty with age.

The Knight of Atri was no different. His hair had grown gray. His sword and shield had rusted. He had sold his horses, hawks, and hounds, his vineyards and his gardens. The old Knight of Atri was content to count the piles of gold coins that he had made from selling everything he owned.

The only thing he kept was the horse who had so often carried him into battle.

But the knight did not take good care of the horse. "Why should I feed this old beast?" the old knight asked. "I hardly use him anymore, so why should I feed him?"

By looking at the old horse, one could tell how poorly the knight cared for him. You could feel the horse's ribs when you touched his sides. His eyes were tired and sad. The poor horse looked old and hungry.

One day the horse went to the knight, begging for a bit of grain or hay to eat.

"It's not a holiday, so I don't see why you should expect to be fed," said the knight. With that, the Knight of Atri turned away his once-favorite horse, and faithful companion.

The tired old horse trudged out into the hot summer sun, his belly begging to eat. The horse wandered through pastures, finding no grass to nibble. The horse wandered through fields, finding no corn to eat. The Knight of Atri's horse finally wandered into the town of Atri, hoping to find something to eat there.

But as the horse walked the streets, food was hard to find. The dogs of the town barked at the horse and chased him. The people shut their doors and windows on this hot day, hoping to keep the heat out. The heat persisted, lulling them to sleep.

The horse spotted the square, where a green vine hung from the Bell of Justice.

The horse hurried to the Bell of Justice. While horses do not know about such things as bells, they *do* know that a green vine can fill an empty stomach.

It was with this knowledge that the hungry horse grabbed the vine that was tied to the Bell of Justice. The vine had been tied to the end of the bell's old, tattered rope rather tightly and the horse could not pull it loose. The horse pulled, and the bell rang.

The bell rang so loudly that all of the people awoke from their naps. They opened their doors and windows, wondering what the ruckus was. They came out, wondering why the Bell of Justice was being rung.

The people went to the bell, where they found the hungry horse munching on the vine. At the front of the crowd stood the judge. Knowing that the horse belonged to the Knight of Atri, the judge sent for him. When the old knight arrived, the judge said:

What good, what honor, what repute
Can come from starving this poor brute?
Therefore I decree that as this steed
Served you in youth, you shall take heed
To comfort his old age, and to provide
Shelter, food, and field beside.

From that day forth, the Knight took care of his horse, and the town never forgot the good that the Bell of Justice could bring.

Casey at the Bat

Written by Ernest Lawrence Thayer
Illustrated by Fiona Sansom

The outlook wasn't brilliant for the Mudville nine that day;
The score stood four to two, with but one inning more to play.
And then when Cooney died at first, and Barrows did the same,
A sickly silence fell upon the patrons of the game.

A straggling few got up to go in deep despair. The rest
Clung to that hope which springs eternal in the human breast;
They thought, if only Casey could but get a whack at that —
We'd put up even money now with Casey at the bat.

But Flynn preceded Casey, as did also Jimmy Blake,
    And the former was a lulu and the latter was a cake;
So upon that stricken multitude grim melancholy sat,
    For there seemed but little chance of Casey's getting to the bat.

But Flynn let drive a single, to the wonderment of all,
    And Blake, the much despised, tore the cover off the ball;
And when the dust had lifted, and the men saw what had occurred,
    There was Jimmy safe at second and Flynn a-hugging third.

Then from 5,000 throats and more there rose a lusty yell;
    It rumbled through the valley, it rattled in the dell;
It knocked upon the mountain and recoiled upon the flat,
    For Casey, mighty Casey, was advancing to the bat.

There was ease in Casey's manner as he stepped into his place;
    There was pride in Casey's bearing and a smile on Casey's face.
And when, responding to the cheers, he lightly doffed his hat,
    No stranger in the crowd could doubt 'twas Casey at the bat.

Ten thousand eyes were on him as he rubbed his hands with dirt;
  Five thousand tongues applauded as he wiped them on his shirt.
Then while the writhing pitcher ground the ball into his hip,
  Defiance flashed in Casey's eye, a sneer curled Casey's lip.

And now the leather-covered sphere came hurtling through the air,
  And Casey stood a-watching it in haughty grandeur there.
Close by the sturdy batsman the ball unheeded sped —
  "That ain't my style," said Casey. "Strike one," the umpire said.

From the benches, black with people, there went up a muffled roar,
    Like the beating of the storm-waves on a stern and distant shore.
"Kill him! Kill the umpire!" shouted someone on the stand;
    It's likely they'd have killed him had not Casey raised his hand.

With a smile of Christian charity great Casey's visage shone;
    He stilled the rising tumult; he bade the game go on;
He signaled to the pitcher, and once more the spheroid flew;
    But Casey still ignored it, and the umpire said, "Strike two."

"Fraud!" cried the maddened thousands, and echo answered fraud;
  But one scornful look from Casey and the audience was awed.
They saw his face grow stern and cold, they saw his muscles strain,
  And they knew that Casey wouldn't let that ball go by again.

The sneer is gone from Casey's lip, the teeth are clenched in hate;
  He pounds with cruel violence his bat upon the plate.
And now the pitcher holds the ball, and now he lets it go,
  And now the air is shattered by the force of Casey's blow.

Oh, somewhere in this favored land the sun is shining bright;

The band is playing somewhere, and somewhere hearts are light,

And somewhere men are laughing, and somewhere children shout;

But there is no joy in Mudville — mighty Casey has struck out.

Jack and the Beanstalk

Adapted from the English fairy tale
Illustrated by John Manders

Once upon a time, there lived a widow and her son, a boy named Jack. Their only possession was a skinny cow. One day, Jack's mother told him to take the cow to town and sell it so they could buy food.

On the way, Jack met a strange man. "I'll trade you these magic beans for your cow," the man said. Jack knew he should sell the cow in town, but he was intrigued by the magic beans.

When Jack returned home, his mother was *not* so thrilled with the beans.

"Who's ever heard of magic beans?! You silly boy, now we'll surely starve!" she yelled. She tossed the beans out the window, and sent her son to bed for the night.

Jack fell asleep feeling bad about what he had done. Of course there was no such thing as a magic bean. What would they eat?

The next morning as Jack rubbed the sleep from his eyes, he saw a giant beanstalk outside his window! The beans *were* magic!

Without a second thought, Jack went outside and began to climb the beanstalk to see where it would lead.

Jack climbed and climbed until he was high among the clouds. He climbed above the clouds at the top of the beanstalk and found himself beneath the most magnificent castle. His curiosity got the best of him, and he decided to see what was inside the castle.

At the tall front door of the castle, Jack found that the keyhole was higher than his head. But he found a way inside through the space at the bottom of the door. As soon as Jack was inside, he heard footsteps crashing toward him and a booming voice that roared:

Fee-fi-fo-fum!
I smell the blood of an Englishman!

Jack looked up, and standing there was a giant—a very angry giant! From the sound of it, the giant was none too happy that Jack was snooping around. Quickly, Jack hid underneath a very large teacup. The giant stopped, and sat at the table with a *THUD!*

"One, two, three, four," said the giant, "I have some, but I want more." Hearing this, and the jingle of coins that came from the table, Jack knew the giant was counting gold.

Soon Jack heard snoring; the giant was asleep! The boy sneaked out from under the cup, took as much gold as he could, and scurried out of the castle. He didn't stop until he was down the beanstalk and back home.

Jack and his mother lived happily for some time, until one day Jack decided to climb back up and explore the castle more. Once there, Jack again heard the giant roar:

Fee-fi-fo-fum!
I smell the blood of an Englishman!

Jack hid behind the table leg. This time the giant pulled out a harp that could sing. The harp sang a lullaby, and soon the giant was asleep. Jack started to take the harp, intending to head back down the beanstalk.

But the harp cried for help, waking the giant. Jack saw the giant running after him.

As Jack climbed down the beanstalk, he yelled, "Hurry, Mother! Bring the hatchet!"

Jack's mother ran to the beanstalk with the hatchet. As Jack reached the ground, he took the hatchet and began to chop at the beanstalk. He looked up as the giant made his way to the ground. Jack kept chopping. The giant was getting closer and closer.

"Hurry," cried his mother. Jack chopped and soon the beanstalk fell to the ground with a *CRASH!*

From that day on, with the giant's gold and magic harp, Jack and his mother lived happily ever after.

Rip Van Winkle

Adapted from the story
by Washington Irving
Illustrated by John Lund

As you journey up the long Hudson River, you will be struck by the beauty of the Catskill Mountains. Rising up to the west, these mountains look different with each change in weather or time of day. When the day is cloudless, the Catskill Mountains hold a misty blanket around themselves, glowing with the rays of the setting sun.

There, magic can take place. A magical thing once happened to a man named Rip Van Winkle, a man well-known in his village at the foot of the Catskill Mountains.

Rip Van Winkle lived in a house he had built with his own two hands. He had a wife who took care of their many children. The children were rosy-cheeked and happy, and they all loved their father. Rip would gather his children around him and play games with them. Late at night around the fireplace, Rip would tell the children stories of mystery and magic. Rip Van Winkle was a good father and a good man who enjoyed his life.

Rip's favorite thing to do was hike among the beautiful Catskill Mountains with his beloved dog. It was on such an evening hike that Rip's famous troubles would occur.

That evening, as Rip and his dog climbed, a strange voice called Rip's name.

"Rip Van Winkle!" the voice cried. "Rip Van Winkle!" It seemed to be getting closer.

Rip looked around, but saw only an old crow perched in a tree. Figuring that his imagination was playing tricks on him, Rip began to hike again. But again the voice called his name, "Rip Van Winkle!"

Rip turned around and spotted a small figure walking toward him. As the stranger came closer, Rip was surprised. The stranger was a short and stout man, with bushy hair and beard. The man carried a barrel. He asked Rip for help, and Rip agreed.

Rip and the man carried the barrel. They went higher into the mountains.

Finally, the two came to a clearing. Here Rip spotted a group of small men much like his new friend. These men were bowling on the grass. The little men all had long, flowing beards and the same funny hats and clothes.

The men opened the barrel, which was full of a dark liquid. Pouring the liquid into mugs, the men offered one to Rip. He found the drink to be so good that he drank mug after mug. The strange little men watched Rip drink. Soon, Rip's head nodded, his eyes closed, and he was sound asleep.

When Rip awoke, he found himself not in the clearing, but lying at the foot of the mountains, where he met the strange man.

"I must have slept here all night long! What will I tell my wife?" Rip thought.

Rip called out to his dog so that they could head home. "Come here, boy!" But Rip's dog would not come.

Rip headed into the village. There, people began to point at Rip. Wondering why they did this, Rip stroked his chin. There he felt a long beard. His clothes were in tatters. The other people were dressed in clothes that seemed strange to Rip. Even the buildings were different, with new paint and signs.

Rip left the village. He walked until he got to where his warm, sturdy home stood. As he came to the house, he expected to hear his wife's voice, scolding him for not coming home the night before. He expected to hear his children playing and his dog barking.

But Rip Van Winkle did not hear his wife or children. And he did not see the house he had left behind the night before. Instead, the house had fallen apart with age.

Then Rip heard a dog bark. But though this dog looked just like Rip's old dog, it was thin and its fur was tangled. It growled at Rip, as if it did not know who he was.

Sad that even his dog was different, Rip wandered back into the village. The people gathered around Rip, still pointing at him. They asked who he was, worried that he was crazy or even dangerous.

A man with a hat hushed the crowd. "Leave this fellow alone," he said. He asked Rip who he was, and why he was there.

"I've lived here my whole life," Rip said.

"Name the people here," the man said.

"Nicholas Vedder, Brom Dutcher ...," Rip told the people of the crowd.

"Nicholas Vedder has been gone for years," said the man. "And Brom Dutcher went off to war."

Rip's heart sank. The changes in his home and friends made him sad. Rip saw a familiar woman. "What is your father's name? Who is your mother?" he asked.

"My father's name was Rip Van Winkle. My mother died of a broken heart because my father left twenty years ago."

"*I* am Rip Van Winkle," Rip said.

The crowd looked closer at Rip. This man *did* look like Rip Van Winkle. He was telling the truth! The man whom they had not seen in twenty years had come home!

That night all the people of the town welcomed Rip home, after twenty long years sleeping in the Catskill Mountains.

The Flying Prince

Adapted from the traditional fairy tale
Illustrated by Kathi Ember

One day, brave Prince Rashar entered a strange forest. A parrot landed on a tree above him, and asked, "Who are you?"

"I am Prince Rashar," said the prince. "I have never seen a talking parrot before."

"Saledra gave me this power," the bird said. "She wanted someone to talk to. Saledra is a beautiful princess. But she is lonely. She lives in the city where day becomes night."

The prince rode off to find this princess.

Soon it became dark. Prince Rashar spotted a campfire. He had entered the camp and found four silly trolls who were fighting.

"What is the trouble?" asked the prince.

"We were digging for mushrooms," said one troll, "and we found these things. This rug flies where you wish. This bag grants wishes. This rope wraps up what it touches." The trolls fought over who kept the treasures.

Prince Rashar came up with a plan. "I will shoot an arrow," he said. "Whichever troll brings it back can keep all of the things."

The trolls ran off to find the arrow. Rashar took the bag and rope. He sat on the rug and said, "Take me to Princess Saledra."

The rug flew over forests and farms. It sailed into the clouds, which blanketed the prince. Prince Rashar soon fell asleep.

He woke up to find himself at the gates of the city where night becomes day. Rashar spotted the gatekeeper. "I need to see Princess Saledra," Prince Rashar said.

"The princess does not leave her castle during the day," said the gatekeeper.

The prince waited for night to fall. Once it was dark, he saw someone walk out onto the castle roof. This someone raised her hand, and light flew from her fingertips. The moon and stars of the night sky shone upon the castle. They lit the face of Princess Saledra!

The princess seemed kind, but sad. "My magic cannot give me what I want," she said. "I wish I had one true friend."

"I will leave the princess a gift!" thought the prince. "I will wait to see if she likes it. If she does, I will meet her."

On the roof, he took out his magic bag.

"Give me a silk robe," he said. "Make it a perfect match for the princess's gown."

Prince Rashar reached inside the bag. Out came a robe! The prince tiptoed into Princess Saledra's room. She was asleep.

"You even look sad as you sleep," Prince Rashar said. "I hope this makes you happy."

He lay the robe on the bed and left.

Princess Saledra found the robe when she awoke. She did not know where it had come from. Someone had brought her a gift!

Prince Rashar flew his rug to the roof again that night. He went into her room and leaned over her.

"Who are you?" the princess asked him.

"I am Prince Rashar," said the prince.

Prince Rashar took Princess Saledra to see his rug. They flew into the night together and did not return until morning.

"You are a true friend, Prince Rashar!" said the princess.

"You are a true friend, too, Princess Saledra," said the prince.

The Selfish Giant

Adapted from the fairy tale by Oscar Wilde
Illustrated by Tammie Lyon

There once was a gorgeous garden with a bed of grass as soft as a pillow. In the garden were scattered tulips and violets and daisies and mums. Peach trees wore pink blossoms in the spring and bore fruit in the fall. Birds filled the garden with their songs.

On their way home, children came to the garden. They lay in the cool grass and hid among the trees. They picked flowers for their mothers and peaches to eat.

One day the Giant returned; this was his garden. The Giant had been away for years, visiting the Ogre. The Giant and the Ogre had talked about all there was to talk about, and the Giant had come home. When he got home, he saw the children in his garden.

"What are you doing playing in my garden?" roared the Giant in a giant voice. The children were frightened and scurried away, dropping their peaches and flowers.

"This is my garden," said the Giant. "Nobody can play in it except me!" The Giant built a wall and put up a sign that said:

TRESPASSERS WILL BE PROSECUTED!

With nowhere else to go, the children spent their days walking around the high garden wall, remembering the fun they used to have inside.

Spring turned to summer and summer became fall and fall gave way to winter. Once winter said farewell, spring came again. Everywhere the children looked, there were birds and blossoms. Everywhere, that is, except in the Selfish Giant's garden.

In the Selfish Giant's garden, it was still winter. The birds refused to sing if there were no children to listen to their songs. The trees refused to blossom if there were no children to climb them and eat their fruit.

The only ones happy with this were Snow and Frost. "Spring has forgotten about the Giant's garden," Snow cheered.

"We can live here forever!" Frost cried.

Snow covered up the grass with her white quilt, and Frost painted the trees silver.

Snow and Frost invited their friends North Wind and Hail to stay with them. The friends were delighted with their new home.

North Wind roared, "I like it here!"

Hail crashed and bashed the roof of the Selfish Giant's castle, calling, "Let me in!"

"Where is Spring?" asked the Selfish Giant, looking at his cold, white garden. "It's awfully late for this sort of weather."

Spring never came to the Selfish Giant's garden, for it did not like selfish people.

Summer did not come to the garden, either, for sunshine and nice weather do not mix well with people who have cold hearts.

Fall filled other gardens with fruit, but passed by the Selfish Giant's garden, saying, "He is too selfish to get anything from me."

It always stayed winter in the Selfish Giant's garden. North Wind, Hail, Frost, and Snow danced through the frosty trees.

One day, the Selfish Giant saw a flower poke through the snow. The flower saw that it was winter, and when it read the Selfish Giant's sign, it crawled back into the ground.

One morning, the Selfish Giant heard lovely music outside. It was just a small bird, chirping outside his window. It had been so long since the Selfish Giant had heard any music at all that it sounded like the most beautiful music in the world.

The Selfish Giant walked outside and found that a small child had slipped through a hole in the garden's high wall.

The trees were so glad to have a child back that they burst into blossoms of pink and white. The birds chirped and cheered with joy. The flowers all peeked out of the ground to see what was going on. Spring had returned and melted the snow and the frost!

Seeing that spring had returned to the Selfish Giant's garden, many children climbed inside. The children rolled in the cool grass. They climbed up the proud peach trees. They picked flowers for their mothers and ripe fruit to eat. The children were so glad that winter had finally melted away.

The Giant's heart melted as well. "How selfish I have been!" he cried. "Children! I am sorry. This is *your* garden now!"

With that, the Giant picked up his giant ax and knocked down the high wall.

From that day on, the Giant would sit in his garden listen to the sound of the birds as they sang, and the children as they played.

Prince Carrots

Adapted from the fairy tale
Illustrated by Kathy Mitchell

Long ago, there were many kings and queens. Their children were princes and princesses. One of these princes was Prince Carrots. He was hard to look at. His head was too wide. His mouth was too big. And he had orange hair. That is why he was called Prince Carrots.

This upset his mother, the queen.

"You must not worry," said Mercury the Magician. "The prince will be intelligent. I can give him a special gift. He can give his intelligence to the person he loves the most."

But every year, the prince's face grew wider. His nose grew longer. His mouth grew bigger. His hair became a brighter orange. But he was very intelligent. The king asked him questions, such as about the Trojan War.

"Helen was kidnapped from Greece by a Trojan named Paris," Prince Carrots said. "Greek soldiers hid in a wooden horse that was taken to the gates of Troy. They spilled out of the horse and attacked Troy to rescue Helen because she was very beautiful."

The queen asked where pearls are from.

"From an oyster," Prince Carrots said. "When sand gets in its shell, it makes a pearl. See, even sand can become beautiful."

Prince Carrots also made people laugh.

"Carrots are good for eyes," he said.

"Except Prince Carrots," was the reply.

Everyone tried not to laugh. It wasn't nice to make fun of the prince, who replied, "Have you ever seen a rabbit with glasses?"

Everyone laughed. The prince smiled.

One day, a princess from a nearby kingdom noticed Prince Carrots' smile.

Prince Carrots was surprised that this princess would look at him, because she was the most beautiful girl he had ever seen.

Prince Carrots could not look away from this beautiful princess. He went to her and introduced himself.

"I am Prince Carrots," he said.

"I am Princess Pia," she said.

"I am honored to meet you," he said.

"I am honored to meet you," she said.

He was shocked. No princess was ever honored to meet him. "I have been told that you are smart," she said. Still, she did not smile. The princess was sad.

"Why are you unhappy?" he asked her.

"I wish I were smart," Pia said.

"But you are very beautiful," he said.

"Yes," she said. "I have heard that a thousand times." Princess Pia told Prince Carrots that she only remembered things if she heard them a thousand times.

"My mother has a magician friend," the princess said. "When I was young, she told him she was worried that I was beautiful but not very smart."

"You *are* beautiful," the prince said.

"But not smart," the princess said. "My mother wanted him to make me intelligent. He told her I would be loved for my beauty."

The prince listened intently.

"My mother was still worried," she said. "The magician told her I would be able to give my beauty to someone. I could give it to the person I loved the most."

The prince nodded again. Princess Pia and he were a lot alike.

The two spent the day together.

Prince Carrots heard the story about Mercury the Magician many times. The princess could not remember that she had already told him.

But Prince Carrots did not mind.

The prince was a good listener. But he was hard to look at. When Pia looked away, he did not seem to mind. She liked that.

The prince loved the way he felt around her. She did not ask questions. She did not expect him to tell jokes. He did not feel ugly when he was with her.

"You are dear to me," the prince said.

"You are dear to me," the princess said.

When they parted, Prince Carrots missed Princess Pia. He wanted to see her.

Princess Pia wanted to see the prince.

"She is lovely even when her hair is tangled," the prince thought.

"He is smart to repeat things so I will remember," the princess thought.

"Will you marry me?" the prince asked.

"Yes!" the princess answered.

Everyone was shocked when they heard the news.

No one could believe it but Mercury the Magician. He knew that we become most what we want to be when we are in love. We are loved for what we truly are.

The Little Dutch Boy

Adapted from the story by Mary Mapes Dodge
Illustrated by Linda Dockey Graves

In the Dutch city of Haarlem, there lived a kind little boy named Hans. His father tended the dikes, or stone walls, that kept the seawater from rushing into Haarlem and washing it away.

One day, Hans's father left for a trip. Since he spent his days watching his father care for the dikes, Hans had nothing to do. "Take this basket of bread to Mr. Jansen," Hans's mother said. Hans happily agreed.

As Hans walked to Mr. Jansen's house,
he passed the dikes. The spring rains had
filled the dikes to the top. His father gone,
Hans wondered who would tend the dikes.

Hans pressed on as it rained. He hunched
his shoulders and pulled his coat tight, trying
to keep the chill out.

Hans pulled his hat down around his
ears. The boy shivered as the cold, hard rain
pelted him, but he kept on walking.

This spring rain was heavier than usual,
pouring down hard day and night. While
the wind turned the windmills, and the rain
watered the tulips, the swollen dikes kept
filling, worrying Hans as he passed.

Hans reached Mr. Jansen's house with the basket of bread. Mr. Jansen was an old man who had no one to care for him. He was one of many sick or poor people whom Hans's mother cared for.

Mr. Jansen was overjoyed that Hans had come. "Sit down," the old man said. "The bread you have brought me smells delicious!"

Hans pulled the bread from the basket and they enjoyed the fresh delights.

Mr. Jansen enjoyed telling the boy his stories about how things were long ago, and about the history of Haarlem and Holland. And Hans loved to listen.

The old man and the boy talked and talked. They laughed and laughed. They ate all of the bread. It was soon very late. Hans didn't realize where the time had gone.

Hans said good night and began the long walk home. He was sad to see that the rain had not let up. "This will make for a cold and wet walk," Hans thought to himself as the rain pattered onto his coat and hat.

The rain began to fall harder. Hans walked faster, the raindrops chilling him. He wanted a warm dinner and his cozy bed.

The rain fell harder and harder. Hans knew that his mother must be worried. Cold and tired, he began to run toward home.

Hans ran and ran, past the tulips and the windmills. His wooden shoes clicked on the brick road and kept his feet warm and dry from the sloshy mud and puddles.

Hans was running when he passed one of the dikes. Something was not right. Hans crept closer to the dike. In a crack between the stone blocks was a small hole. From the hole seeped a small trickle of water.

While the water looked harmless, Hans knew that the water behind the wall would push at the tiny hole until it became bigger. Soon the water would rush through, washing away the town. Hans stuck his fist into the hole, plugging it up.

Hans stood at the leaking dike with his fist stuck in the hole, his hand the only thing keeping the water from washing away the town of Haarlem.

Hans's mother did not know the trouble that her son had discovered. She did not know that he was stuck in the storm, soaked to the bone from the rain.

"Hans!" she called from the door of their house. "Hans, where are you?"

If only her husband were home, she thought. He would bravely venture into the storm and find their beloved son. Little did she know that Hans was showing bravery of his own.

The rain pelted Hans, and the wind swirled. But the boy kept his hand in the hole. He knew that to save his town, he could not let the water through the dike.

Hans was so cold. He shivered and shook. His hand was tired and numb. But he couldn't leave the dike.

"Help!" Hans called out.

The wind drowned out Hans's cries. He was sure nobody had heard him.

Suddenly, there was old Mr. Jansen.

"I heard you, Hans," the old man said. He picked up a stone and plugged the hole.

"Let's get you home," said Mr. Jansen, "Then I'll tell how you saved the town!"

Ali Baba

Adapted from the traditional folktale
Illustrated by Anthony Lewis

In ancient times, there lived a poor woodcutter named Ali Baba. Ali Baba spent his days splitting wood.

One day Ali Baba was working in the woods when he heard horse hooves. He saw a group of fearsome men coming his way. He climbed into a tree to watch the men.

Forty men stopped at a cave. Each man carried a heavy sack.

The leader got off his horse and said, "Open sesame." The cave's rock door opened and the men carried their sacks into the cave.

When the forty men came back out of the cave, they were not carrying the heavy, jingling sacks. The leader of the group said, "Close sesame," and the door slammed shut.

Ali Baba hid until the men rode off. Curious as to what was inside the cave, Ali Baba said to the door, "Open sesame."

Ali Baba walked into the cave. It was full of treasure! There were gold statues and Persian rugs. There were pieces of pottery and sacks of coins. Ali Baba saw the forty heavy sacks that the men had carried. He carried out as many sacks as he could and said, "Close sesame," to shut the cave's door.

But Ali Baba had left his ax in the cave.

Ali Baba arrived home with the money. He would never have to cut wood again!

Using the money, Ali Baba bought a shop in the marketplace. He hired a friend, Morgiana, to tend the shop. Morgiana was a clever woman, and loyal to Ali Baba.

However, the men whose money he had taken were thieves and robbers. The forty thieves returned to their cave to find the money missing and an ax left behind.

The leader said, "We must go to the city and find which woodcutter this ax belongs to. That is where we will find our gold."

The thieves went to the city. One of them went to the marketplace—to Ali Baba's shop.

"Who owns this shop?" the man asked.

"Ali Baba," Morgiana said. "He bought it with money he found."

The man returned to the thieves' cave.

Knowing who had taken his money, the leader had a plan. He told the thief who had found the shop to put an X on its door, so the thieves knew which shop to break into.

The thief went into town and put an X on the shop's door. But he didn't realize that he was spotted by Morgiana. The clever woman waited until the thief left, and then marked an X on every shop door on the street.

The band of thieves could not tell which shop was Ali Baba's.

"Someone foiled my plan!" shouted the leader. "I have a new plan that won't fail."

The next night, he disguised himself. He had the thieves take twenty mules and put two oil barrels on each. The other thieves climbed into the barrels, and their leader led the mules to Ali Baba's shop.

At Ali Baba's door stood a man with twenty mules. "I am an oil merchant," the man said. "I want to sell you some fine oil."

"Please come inside," said Ali Baba. "You may put your mules in my stable."

The leader took the mules to the stable and whispered to the thieves, "When I whistle, run to the shop and attack Ali Baba."

Morgiana was also at Ali Baba's shop. She made tea for the visitor. Alas, the stove was out of oil. Morgiana had seen the barrels of oil that the merchant had brought and went to borrow a bit. She went to the stable.

Morgiana heard a voice from inside one barrel. "Is it time to attack?" the voice asked.

"No, not yet," Morgiana replied.

Then Morgiana took straw from the floor and set it on fire. She lifted the lid of each oil barrel and threatened to throw the burning straw in. Thieves popped out and ran away.

Hearing the commotion of the frightened thieves, their leader came outside. His plan foiled, he ran, too.

The leader was angry at the failure of his plan. The thirty-nine thieves never returned to the cave. "I'll take Ali Baba's money all for myself," the leader said.

This time the leader donned a different disguise. He dressed as a fellow shop owner on Ali Baba's street. Ali Baba invited the man home, not seeing the knife in the man's robe.

But Morgiana saw the knife. That night, she was the dinner entertainment. She danced and waved silk scarves. She used the scarves to tie up the thief and take his knife.

"Thank you for stopping that thief," said Ali Baba. "I am making you a partner at my shop!" And that is exactly what happened.

Pecos Bill

Adapted from the American legend
Illustrated by Mike Spoor

ore than a hundred years ago in the Wild West, Pecos Bill was born.

When Pecos Bill was a baby, his parents moved from one ranch to another. Bill was asleep in the back of their wagon when it hit a bump. The bump bumped Bill out of the wagon and onto the desert ground. Bill's parents had no idea, and kept on riding.

A family of coyotes found the boy and raised him as their own. Pecos Bill learned to live in the hot desert. Each night, Bill and his coyote family howled at the moon.

Once Pecos Bill was a man, he left his coyote family and went to live with people. As a cowboy, Bill had many adventures.

Pecos Bill's first adventure was the time when he rode Widow-Maker. Widow-Maker was a horse, but not just any horse. He was the roughest, meanest horse any cowboy had ever ridden—or tried to ride. Nobody could stay on Widow-Maker. He was too ornery.

Whenever a cowboy got the nerve to climb onto Widow-Maker's back, that big black stallion would buck and kick. He would snort and stomp and toss his head. Pretty soon, he would toss that poor cowboy out of the saddle and onto the dry, dusty desert dirt.

No cowboy ever had what it took to ride Widow-Maker — except for Pecos Bill.

One day Bill watched Widow-Maker toss one cowboy after another onto the dirt and decided he'd seen enough. "Why don't I show you boys how it's done?" he asked.

Pecos Bill climbed onto Widow-Maker's back and the rest of the cowboys held their breath, waiting for Widow-Maker to toss Bill.

Widow-Maker bucked and kicked. He snorted and stomped and tossed his head. But Pecos Bill wasn't tossed anywhere. Hanging on tight, Bill tired Widow-Maker out. That horse had met his match — and now he had a new master.

The taming of Widow-Maker was not the only adventure Pecos Bill had. You know how cowboys use a looped rope called a lasso?

When Pecos Bill was tending his cattle, the herd stampeded. The cows were getting away, and Bill had forgotten his lasso at home. Thinking quickly, Pecos Bill caught a few rattlesnakes, and tied them together. With the rattling, hissing lasso, Pecos Bill roped that whole herd of cattle just like that!

Once Pecos Bill was tending his cattle and heard a roar from the tumbleweed. Bill saw a mountain lion ready to sink its fangs and claws into one of the cows.

Bill wasn't about to let some mangy kitty cat take one of his heifers, so he roped the mountain lion just like he would a pony. Then Bill climbed on the cat's back and began to whoop and holler, "You like that, pussycat?"

Yes, Pecos Bill sure was the rootin-est, tootin-est cowpoke to climb into the saddle in the Wild West.

Pecos Bill had many adventures in the Wild West. There wasn't a horse he couldn't ride. There wasn't a challenge that could stop him. But one day Pecos Bill met his match. Her name was Slue-Foot Sue.

Slue-Foot Sue was the prettiest girl this side of the Mississippi River. Her hair was as golden as Kansas wheat. Her cheeks were as rosy as an Arizona sunset.

Pecos Bill had never felt the slightest fear when riding an angry bull or facing a nest of rattlers. But moseying up to Slue-Foot Sue made Bill more nervous than a jackrabbit in a wolf den. Luckily, Sue introduced herself and before you know it, the two were married.

Married life didn't tame Pecos Bill. One time a twisting cyclone tried to fly off with Bill's herd. But just like he wouldn't let a mountain lion touch one of his cows, Pecos Bill wasn't about to let an old cyclone, either.

Pecos Bill got out his lasso and tossed it around the cyclone. Off it flew, trying to throw Bill south of the Rio Grande. Our hero held on tight, and soon that cyclone petered out. Pecos Bill had triumphed once again!

Speaking of the Rio Grande, you know what a long and winding river it is. Well, Pecos Bill lassoed that big river and used it to water the crops he grew on his ranch! That Pecos Bill sure was a son of a gun!

Through his long and exciting life, Pecos Bill had more adventures, with earthquakes and rattlesnakes, with grizzly bears and stampeding steers and fleet-footed deer. He had so many wild and woolly adventures it would fill this whole book to tell them.

As the years passed, Pecos Bill and Slue-Foot Sue grew old and gray. Bill still tended his cattle, and he still rode Widow-Maker, who had grown a little gray himself.

But after a long day, Pecos Bill would feel sorer than when he was young. So he was happy to sit with Slue-Foot Sue and watch the sun set on the spread they called home. And that is the story of Pecos Bill.

Paradise

Adapted from the Grimm's fairy tale
Illustrated by Amy Flynn

om and Lucy lived on a farm, but they did not have much. They had a plow, a tractor, and an old hen named Madge. The name of their farm was Paradise.

"It doesn't feel like paradise," Tom said.

Tom could not grow the corn by himself. Lucy tried to plow, but the plow got stuck. She tried to plant, but the seeds blew away. She tried to pick the corn, but pulled too hard. More corn needed to be planted.

"We'll have to sell Madge," Tom said.

Lucy set off with Madge under her arm.

Lucy walked and walked. Madge cackled and squawked. They reached the bird farm.

Madge flew from Lucy's arms and across the barnyard. Lucy ran after her.

Madge flew through a puddle. Lucy fell in the puddle. Mud splashed all over her.

Madge flew through the goose pen. Lucy followed her. Geese honked at them.

Madge flew through the duck pen. Lucy followed her. Ducks quacked at them.

Madge flew through the turkey pen. She flew through the peacock pen. Lucy tripped on a turkey. She flipped over a peacock.

Madge flew down the road toward Paradise. Lucy ran after her.

Back at the farm, Tom heard Madge squawk. He saw her coming down the road. A strange creature was running after Madge.

This strange creature was as large as a person. It had goose feathers on its head and duck feathers on its arms and turkey feathers on its belly. Behind it were peacock feathers.

The strange creature looked up at Tom. It opened its mouth to speak.

"I didn't sell Madge," it said. "But look at all the lovely feathers I brought back."

"Lucy? Is that you?" Tom asked.

"Yes," she said. "I don't think Madge wants to be sold."

Tom set off with Madge under his arm.

Tom walked. Madge squawked. They came to a house where a woman stood. She raised a cup over her head and counted to ten. "Full!" she said. She slapped her hand over the cup and ran inside the house.

"Oh, no!" Tom heard the woman cry.

She came back outside, looking sad.

"Howdy," Tom said. "I'm from a place called Paradise. Do you need help?"

"I'm trying to take sunshine into my kitchen," the woman said. "Sunshine flows into the cup when I'm outside. I put my hand over the cup and then I run inside. But when I lift my hand, it is gone. I'll give you one hundred dollars to bring sunshine inside."

Tom took an ax and chopped a hole in her wall. "Now you have a window," he said.

"I wanted a window," the woman said. "I was afraid it would be too much work."

She handed Tom one hundred dollars.

Tom put the money in his pocket. He set off down the road, Madge under his arm.

They came to another house. A man tried to put on a shirt. His arms were in the sleeves, but there was no hole for his head.

"Howdy," Tom said. "I come from a place called Paradise. Do you need help?"

"Yes, I do," the man said. "I want to wear this shirt. But I can't get it over my head. I'd give two hundred dollars to wear this shirt."

"You want to wear this shirt?" Tom asked. He took scissors, snipped a hole in the top, and said, "Now you have a neck hole."

"I wanted a neck hole," the man said. "I was afraid it would be too much work."

He handed Tom two hundred dollars.

Tom put the money in his pocket. He set off down the road, Madge under his arm.

They came upon another house. A woman was crying into a handkerchief.

"Howdy," Tom said. "I come from a place called Paradise. Do you need help?"

"Paradise?" she asked. "You are just the man I wanted to see," she said. "I'd give three hundred dollars for a new suit."

"Go to town and buy one," Tom said.

"My husband was buried in his work clothes," the woman said. "I wanted him to have a suit, but it would be too much work. I don't want him wearing work clothes in Paradise. You're from Paradise. Give him this money to buy a new suit?" She handed Tom three hundred dollars.

Tom put the money in his pocket. He set off down the road, Madge under his arm.

"Those people were all alike," he thought. "They were afraid of work. Now I can buy seed and don't have to sell Madge!"

Tom had money in his pocket, a chicken, and a wife he loved. This was Paradise!

Rikki-Tikki-Tavi

*Adapted from the story
by Rudyard Kipling
Illustrated by Richard Bernal*

Rikki-tikki-tavi once won a battle in the big bungalow. His feathered friend Darzee lent a hand, but Rikki-tikki-tavi won the battle by himself. This is his story.

Rikki-tikki-tavi was a mongoose, a small animal that has the fur and tail of a cat and the head and fierceness of a weasel.

One day, a flood came through the hole that Rikki-tikki-tavi shared with his family. The flood carried the mongoose down the road, where a small boy found him. The boy, named Teddy, took Rikki-tikki-tavi home.

Teddy showed the wet little mongoose to his parents. "Is it dead?" he asked his father.

Teddy's father picked up Rikki-tikki-tavi, and said, "No, this mongoose is alive. But he seems to be choked from the water."

Teddy's mother brought a towel into the kitchen and wrapped Rikki-tikki-tavi in it. Warm and dry, the little mongoose opened his eyes and let out a wet mongoose sneeze.

Rikki-tikki-tavi began to look around, as members of the mongoose family are curious. He sniffed at Teddy and gave the boy a lick.

"Oh, my," said Teddy's father, "I think he's so friendly because you saved his life."

"Can we keep him?" Teddy asked.

"What if he bites?" asked Teddy's mother.

"Rubbish!" announced Teddy's father. "If ever a snake came into Teddy's bedroom, this little fellow could take care of it."

Snakes and mongooses are enemies. Mongooses are one of the few animals that can win a fight with a snake. It wouldn't be long before Rikki-tikki-tavi had his first.

One day Rikki-tikki-tavi was with his friend, Darzee, when they heard a rustle.

"Oh, no," said Darzee. "It's Nag!"

"Who is Nag?" Rikki-tikki-tavi asked.

"I am Nag," said a large, red-eyed cobra that came slithering from the brush.

"Be afraid!" hissed Nag.

But Rikki-tikki-tavi was not afraid, for his mother had fed him cobras when he was young. He knew that the life of a mongoose was spent catching snakes like Nag.

That night, Rikki-tikki-tavi was in the bungalow when he heard a noise. He spotted Nag and his cobra wife, Nagaina.

"We must empty this house of people," Nagaina said.

"Yes," agreed Nag. "If we get rid of the people, then the mongoose cannot stay."

"Bite the boy's father first," Nagaina told her husband. "Then get me, and together we shall beat that little mongoose."

With Nagaina gone, Rikki-tikki-tavi saw his chance. Jumping, he lunged at Nag.

"No!" screamed Nag, mongoose teeth poking his head. The cobra thrashed, trying to shake the little mongoose off.

But Rikki-tikki-tavi held on tight. If he had let go, Nag could have bitten him.

The snake and the mongoose thrashed and crashed around the bathroom.

Suddenly there was a loud *THUD!* Rikki-tikki-tavi noticed that the cobra had stopped fighting. He looked up to see Teddy's father holding a broomstick. With the man's help, Rikki-tikki-tavi had defeated the deadly and vicious cobra, Nag.

"Bad Nag is gone, gone, gone," Rikki-tikki-tavi heard someone sing. It was Darzee.

"Where's Nagaina?" the mongoose asked.

"She is at the garbage pile, crying for her husband," Darzee said. "She has a nest of eggs that will hatch and become cobras."

"Where is this nest?" Rikki-tikki-tavi asked the bird. Darzee told him.

"You must pretend that your wing is hurt, in order to lure Nagaina away from her nest. Then I will steal away all of her eggs. Once I take care of Nagaina, we will be safe," Rikki-tikki-tavi said to the bird.

The bird and the mongoose headed off, hoping that their plan would work.

Darzee distracted Nagaina. This let Rikki-tikki-tavi get rid of the eggs. Nagaina did not realize until only one egg was left.

Quickly, she grabbed the last egg and tried to escape. She found a hole to crawl into and was just about inside when...

... Rikki-tikki-tavi grabbed her by the tail. "Drop that egg, Nagaina!" he yelled.

Nagaina pulled Rikki-tikki-tavi down into the hole. By this time, Teddy and his family were watching. They were worried that their pet was gone.

But just when all hope had been lost, Rikki-tikki-tavi climbed from the hole. He was safe, and now so was his family!

The Seal's Skin

Adapted from the traditional Scottish folktale
Illustrated by Linda Dockey Graves

ean was a fisherman. He spent his days at sea. The work was easy for Sean. He was born to fish. But he was lonely.

The fishing boats returned to the docks each night. They sorted through the fish. They folded up the nets. They hurried up to the village and met their waiting families.

Sean walked home alone along the rocky shore. Smoke rose from cottage chimneys. Families were inside. Sean did not have a wife or a family. His cottage was dark, cold, and empty. He was not happy.

Life on land was too slow for Sean.
He liked to fish — even at night.

"The sea has magic and mystery," his
father had said. Sean had heard the legends
many times. He had heard about mermaids,
magical serpents, and sea sprites. They lived
in an undersea world. They rarely showed
themselves to the people of the land.

Sean's father used to tell him about the
selkies. His father said that some seals were
regular people under their skins. They could
remove their smooth skins like clothes.

Sean's father used to point to the seals.
"Look at how big and round their eyes are,"
he used to say. "They look like human eyes."

As Sean walked one night, he heard noises. Hiding, Sean saw three women.

They danced on a rock beside the waves and sang with clear voices. They were the most beautiful women he had ever seen.

Sean climbed toward them. He stepped on something soft. He picked it up.

The women ran across the rocks. Two of them slipped into seal skins. They slid off the rock and into the tide. The third woman ran to Sean. She saw her soft skin in his hands.

"You can return my skin or dress me," she said. "If you return my skin, you will never see me again. If you give me clothes, I will be your wife."

Sean held the seal skin close. "You are a seal?" he asked the beautiful woman.

"I am a seal when I am in the skin," she said. "When I am not, I'm a person like you."

Sean put his coat around the woman to keep her warm. "I will give you a wonderful life here on land," he said. "You will have a house in the village. You will have children. You will have everything you want or need."

Sean looked into her eyes and said, "But you must promise to stay here forever. You must never return to your life in the sea."

"I promise," she said. "Take the skin, and lock it away. I will wear a dress instead."

Sean knew he would marry this woman.

Sean took her to his cottage. She warmed herself by the fire, and Sean hid the seal skin in a chest. Then he hid the key to the chest.

The woman asked Sean many questions about life in the village.

"People love their families," Sean said. "Children are important. Work is important. Singing and dancing are also important."

"It is the same with the people of the sea," the woman said. "We love our families. We work. We sing and dance."

"You will need a name," said Sean.

"I have a name," she said. "It is Mara."

Mara knew this new life on land would be an adventure.

Mara loved her life on land. And she loved Sean. She also loved the people of the village, learning their names and customs.

She learned the stories they told.

"It is strange," she said. "The villagers tell stories about the people of the sea. We tell stories about the people of the land."

Soon, Sean and Mara had a daughter named Sela. She had large, round eyes like her mother. She also loved the sea.

Years passed. Mara and Sela would wave to Sean as he rowed out to sea.

Mara looked out over the ocean. She missed her people. She missed the sea. One day, Sean came home to find Mara crying.

Why are you crying?" Sean asked.

"I love you and Sela," Mara said. "But I miss my family. I miss the people of the sea."

"We are your family," said Sean.

"I am sorry," Mara said. "I was not meant to live on land. I need to swim in the tides."

Sean pulled an old, rusty key from his pocket. Then he put it in Mara's hand. Mara held the key. She kissed Sean.

The seal skin was inside the chest. Mara put it on and splashed into the water.

Sean and Sela walked along the shore every night. Sean told her stories of the sea.

As they walked, a seal would appear. They knew it was Mara by her beautiful eyes.

Stone Soup

Adapted from the traditional folktale
Illustrated by Barbara Lanza

ack Grand walked along with a feather in his hat, and a smile on his face.

Jack Grand was a rat-a-tat man. He could do all sorts of things. He could dance. He could walk on his hands. He could yodel. He could hum. He could play the drum. He could whittle. He even knew riddles.

Jack had a good life. But often, he was hungry. He had not eaten in many days. He walked until he saw a village. "Where there's a village, there are people. Where there are people, there is food," Jack thought.

Jack came upon a house. A name was painted on the gate: TUBBS. An old man opened the door. Jack bowed and said, "I'm Jack Grand, the rat-a-tat man."

"I have no money," said Mr. Tubbs.

"I understand," Jack said. "I'm hungry."

"I only have salt and pepper," said Mr. Tubbs. "Ask Miss Grubbs next door."

A thin lady answered at the next house.

"Hello, Miss Grubbs," Jack said. "I'm Jack Grand, the rat-a-tat man."

"I have no money," said Miss Grubbs.

"The truth is," Jack said, "I'm hungry."

"I have only a head of garlic," said Miss Grubbs. "Ask Mrs. Chubbs next door."

A plump woman answered at the next house. Jack said, "Hello, Mrs. Chubbs, I'm Jack Grand, the rat-a-tat man."

"I have no money," said Mrs. Chubbs.

"I'm so hungry," Jack said.

"I have only a few potatoes," said Mrs. Chubbs. "Ask someone else."

Jack knocked on every door. One woman had only cabbage. Her neighbor had only carrots. One family had only a bit of bacon. Another family had only a handful of beans.

Jack walked along for a while. He saw a stone. The stone gave Jack an idea.

He picked it up and examined it. "Perfect," Jack said to himself.

Jack ran back to town. He knocked on the first door. Mr. Tubbs answered.

"You have no food to share," Jack said. "But do you have a big pot I could borrow?"

"A big pot?" asked Mr. Tubbs. "What have you got there, son?"

"It's a soup stone," Jack said.

"A soup stone?" asked Mr. Tubbs.

"To make soup," Jack said.

Mr. Tubbs came out with a big pot.

Jack carried the big pot to the village square. He filled it with water. He built a fire underneath it and dropped the stone in.

The pot bubbled. Jack dipped his spoon into the water. He tasted it. "Perfect," he said.

"It would be better with a little salt and pepper," said Jack, "Not much. Just a little."

"I have salt and pepper," said Mr. Tubbs. He ran to his cottage and returned with a salt shaker and a pepper mill.

Jack sprinkled the salt into the pot. He ground the pepper into the pot. It bubbled. Jack dipped his spoon into the pot and tasted the soup. "Perfect," he said.

Miss Grubbs came out of her cottage. She had been watching Jack. She came over and peeked into the pot.

"It's stone soup," said Mr. Tubbs.

"Is it good?" asked Miss Grubbs.

"It would be better with a little garlic," said Jack, "Not much. Just a little."

"I have garlic," said Miss Grubbs. She ran to her cottage and returned with garlic.

Jack chopped the head of garlic. He sprinkled the garlic into the pot and stirred.

The pot bubbled. Jack dipped his spoon into the pot. He tasted the stone soup. "Perfect," he said.

Mrs. Chubbs came out of her cottage. She had been watching Jack, too. She came over and peeked into the pot, curious as to what it was.

"It's stone soup," said Miss Grubbs.

"Is it any good?" asked Mrs. Chubbs.

Just as Mr. Tubbs and Miss Grubbs had done, Mrs. Chubbs brought an apron full of potatoes, which Jack added to the pot.

Soon, the entire village had gathered. They wanted to know what was in the pot.

A woman ran to get cabbage. A man ran to get carrots. Other villagers ran to get beans and bacon. Jack threw it all into the pot.

Jack spooned soup for everyone. He ate until he was full. The villagers ate until they were full. They ate until the pot was empty.

Empty, that is, except for the stone.

"Use it for your next pot of stone soup," Jack said to the villagers as he headed to another village to meet more new friends.

The Golden Goose

Adapted from the Grimm's fairy tale
Illustrated by Karen Dugan

Once a log cabin stood in a forest. It was home to a boy named Samuel. He lived with his mother, father, and two older brothers. Samuel tried not to make trouble. He did what he was told. But his family always found fault with him.

"Who will chop wood?" his mother asked one day. Samuel did not offer to go.

"I will go," Samuel's brother Tom said.

"Good boy," said their mother.

Soon Tom returned home. He had his ax and his lunch basket. He did not have any wood. His shoulder was bleeding.

"What happened?" their mother asked.

"I met a strange man in the woods," Tom said. "He was old. He asked for food. He wanted to get his dirty hands on my lunch!"

"What did you tell him?" Samuel asked.

"I told him no!" Tom said. "I said there were only enough cakes for me. I ordered him to leave. Then I began chopping wood. I lost my hold on the ax and cut my shoulder."

"I will go chop the wood," said Samuel's other brother, Jack.

"Good boy," said their mother.

Soon Jack returned home, carrying his lunch basket. He did not have the ax. He did not have any wood. His foot was bleeding.

"What happened?" their mother asked.

"I went to finish Tom's work," Jack said. "That old man was there. He asked for a drink. He wanted to get his lips on my jug!"

"What did you tell him?" Samuel asked.

"I told him no!" Jack said. "I said there was only enough lemonade for me."

"Did you get hurt, too?" asked Samuel.

"Yes," Jack said. "The ax broke and cut my foot. The man stood there, laughing."

"I will go chop the wood," Samuel said.

His family stared at him and laughed.

Samuel was not afraid. He saw the ax on the ground and the old man nearby.

"I am Samuel," he said. "You have met my brothers. I am sorry they were rude."

"Will you sit?" the old man asked.

Samuel could see the man was very old and wrinkled. His skin looked like walnut shells. But he seemed nice. His hands were not dirty. His lips were not wormy.

"I am very thirsty and hungry," the man said. "Will you share your lunch with me?"

Samuel untied his cloth. It was filled with sweet cakes and a jug of lemonade.

"What luck!" Samuel said. "Surely we will eat well!"

"You are not like your brothers," said the old man. "You shared your lunch with me. You kept me company before chopping wood. You are a kind young man."

Samuel did not know what to say. He was not used to hearing nice words.

"I will repay your kindness," said the man. "See the tree with the ax marks in it?"

Samuel nodded.

"I kept your brothers from chopping that tree down," said the old man. "Look inside the tree. You will find something."

The man started down the road. Samuel began to chop at the tree. Inside the stump he found a goose with golden feathers!

Samuel could not take the goose home, where his unkind family would take it away.

Samuel started toward town. He held onto the goose. He passed other travelers. He noticed their stares and whispers.

But the people were not talking about Samuel. They were talking about the goose.

Three sisters saw the goose. The eldest sister reached out to see if it was real.

The younger girls grabbed their sister to stop her, just as the eldest girl touched the goose. They became stuck, too!

A judge grabbed the last girl. He was stuck, too. The girls' mother grabbed the judge's coat, and also became stuck.

Samuel led the growing line of people into town. He had heard of a sad princess who lived at the palace. She would not smile. Samuel wanted to give her the goose. The king had promised half his land to whoever made his daughter smile.

The king and the princess watched as Samuel and his parade of stuck people passed. The judge and sisters and mother all bickered and tugged as Samuel approached.

The princess, seeing this crazy parade, began to smile. She laughed until tears fell from her eyes. She could not stop.

Samuel married her, and the two lived and laughed together from that day forth.

Good Night!